let's look at my home

Nicola Tuxworth

LORENZ BOOKS

Kitchen

Food is stored and cooked in the kitchen.

cups

crisp vegetables

rolling pin

saucepan

trash can

oven mitt

shiny
colander

bowl

making tasty
sandwiches

frying pan

oven

wooden
spoon

apron

Dining room

The dining room is a special place for eating meals.

knife

napkin

fruit

fork

spoon

glass

bread board

placemat

eating lunch together

plate

crusty
bread

spotted water jug

Baby's room

Sometimes babies sleep in a room of their own.

teddy bear

baby bottle

elephant mobile

diaper

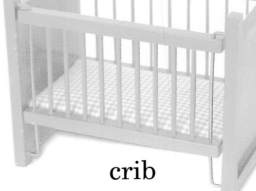

crib

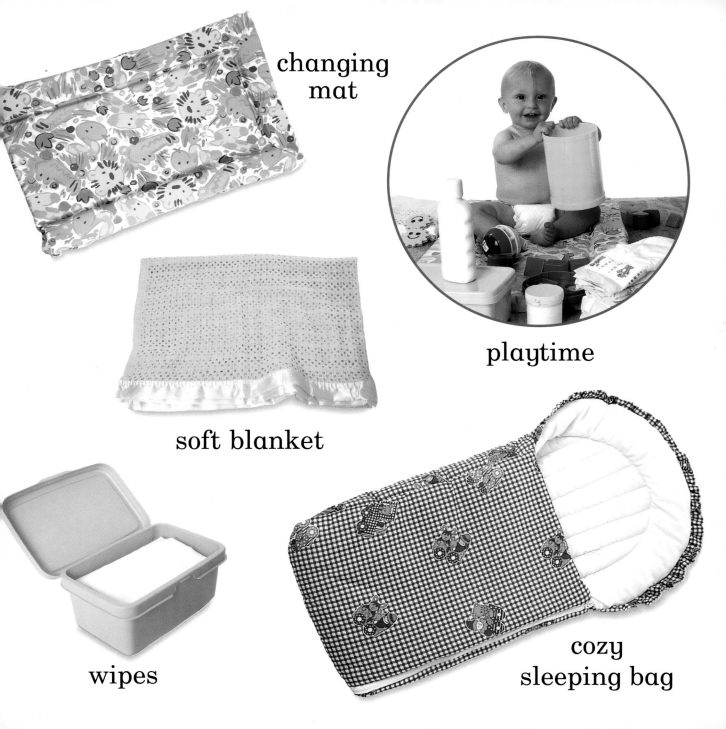

changing
mat

playtime

soft blanket

wipes

cozy
sleeping bag

Bathroom

The bathroom is where we clean ourselves.

mirror

hairbrush

soft towel

toy boats

bath

soap

bath duck

toothpaste

bathtime fun

toothbrush

potty

smiley
bath sponge

Living room

The living room is a comfortable place to relax in.

potted plant

books

coffee table

rug

table lamp

soft
cushion

reading together

flowers

squishy bean bag

photograph

Playroom

You can paint, draw
or play with your
toys in a playroom.

dump
truck

paint box

jigsaw puzzle

doll

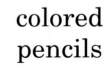

colored
pencils

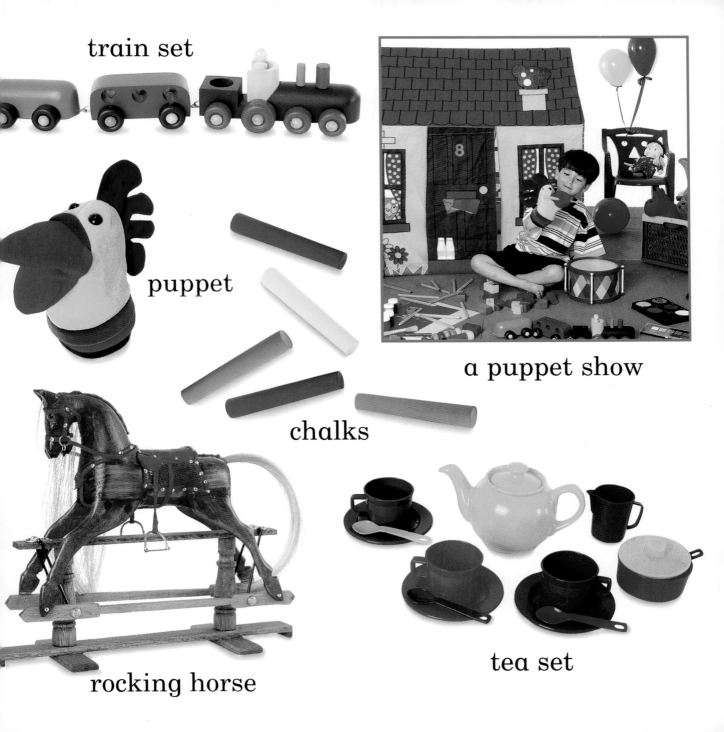

train set

puppet

a puppet show

chalks

rocking horse

tea set

Bedroom

The bedroom is where you go to rest and sleep.

slippers

cuddly dinosaurs

robe

book shelf

pajama
case

sleep tight

teddy bear
clock

waste
basket

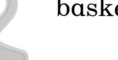

coat hanger

chair

In the garden

Lots of people grow flowers in the garden.

twine

trowel

potting compost

seeds

broom

wheelbarrow

roses

watering the plants

bike

flowerpot

Toolshed

The toolshed is full of tools for grown-ups to use in the home.

pots of paint

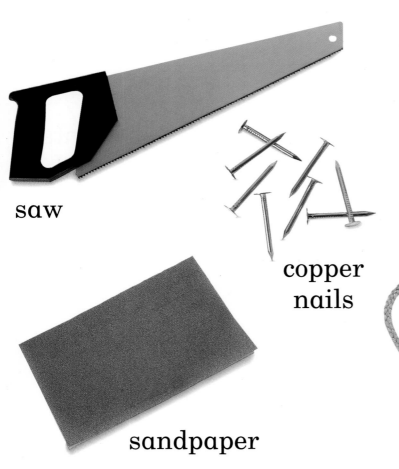

saw

copper nails

sandpaper

rope

nut

bolt

fixing things
with toy tools

silver
nails

screwdriver

step
ladder

hammer

Where do they go?